Jessica and the Lost Stories

Jenny Nelson

ILLUSTRATED BY ALICE PRIESTLEY

DANCING SUN BOOKS, *an imprint of*
gage EDUCATIONAL PUBLISHING COMPANY
A DIVISION OF CANADA PUBLISHING CORPORATION
TORONTO ONTARIO CANADA

For Jessica, of course.

Copyright © 1992 Gage Educational Publishing Company

A Division of Canada Publishing Corporation

Canadian Cataloguing in Publication Data

Nelson, Jenny, 1947-
  Jessica and the lost stories

"Dancing sun books".
ISBN 0-7715-6953-X

I. Priestley, Alice. II. Title.

PS8577.E5TJ4 1991   jC813'.54   C91-095172-1
PZ7.N45Je 1991

Design: Mary Opper

ISBN 0-7715-**6953-X**

1 2 3 4 5 FP 95 94 93 92 91

Written, Printed, and Bound in Canada

Moon Riddle

On the shore of an island in the western sea,
    When the moon shone full and the sea shone silver,
In a cabin on an island in the western sea,
    When the moon shone full and the beach shone silver.
      Where have they gone?
        When is the time?
When the moon shines full and the sea shines silver.

On a far island in the western sea lived a young
girl named Jessica. She lived with her mother and
father and baby sister in a little cabin on a big beach.
The cabin sat between the forest and the sea.

There were no other children living nearby,
but Jessica had lots to do. She helped her father
bake cookies. She helped her mother pack wood.
She drew pictures in the sand with spiky beach grass.
She played with the shells and the waves and the wind.
And she had her stories.

Jessica was a Storyteller.

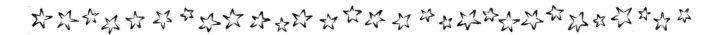

She told such funny stories
that she could make even a
grumbly grumbletoes giggle.

She told very scary stories
that sometimes hung around long
past bedtime.

She told glad stories and sad stories,
tall tales and small tales.

But one night, something very odd happened
to Jessica's stories.

It was a night when the moon shone full,
as round and fat and shiny as a big glass ball.

Outside the cabin, shadows lay long
across the moon-white sand.

7

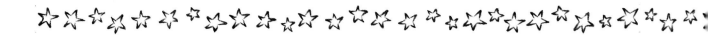

Inside the cabin, Jessica's family were gathered near the warm, wood stove. It was time for the bedtime story. Jessica settled into her favourite storytelling chair. Her mother and father and baby sister moved closer to listen. Jessica began, "Once upon a full moon night,…"

And that's when it happened. Jessica lost her stories. She opened her mouth. But no more story came out. She thought and she thought and she thought. It was no use. There were no stories in her head at all.

Jessica hopped up. She looked all over the cabin.
She looked under the cat and under the bed.
She could not find her stories.

She looked in the teacup cupboard and in her
toothbrush cup. No stories.

She looked through the window.
She saw the big moon and the silver sea.
Then she heard a tiny giggle way up in the sky,
and she knew.

Jessica wasn't sure when or why or how.
She just knew, that's all. Her stories had wandered
lost through the dark trees, and flown up to the
moon. Jessica's stories were all up on the moon.

Well, it wasn't long before Jessica began to miss her stories very much. Everything seemed so dull.

It was like finding a box,
without wanting to know what was
hidden inside.

It was like being a star
without a sparkle, or a train
without a toot.

All the strange creatures and magic and bright colours had flown away. Jessica couldn't remember what a princess wore, or if trees ever talk, or where a boat might go.

Every day
Jessica felt sadder and sadder,
but the stories did not
come back.

And every night Jessica went outside to look up at the moon.

At first the moon was hardly there at all. It looked like a thin slice of lemon, just the thin yellow smile of a moon.

Jessica waited.

The nights got colder, and the moon got fatter.

It grew to the size of a half-eaten cookie.

Jessica knew that the moon would keep growing.
So she waited and she waited and she watched.

Sure enough, one evening when she gazed up at the sky, the moon was full. It floated in the dark as round and flat and shiny as a big glass ball. Beneath the moon the sea shone silver.

Jessica decided that very night to go and visit the moon and find her lost stories.

She packed a thermos of hot mint tea and honey, and put a handful of cookies in her pocket. She put on her nice, warm sweater and her big, blue tuque. Then she waved goodbye to the cabin, and set out.

It was quite bright outside, because the moon was so big and bright. She walked along the beach. White shells lit up in the sand. Sea waves rolled in, edged with silver.

Jessica stopped. There, floating in the water, was the moon. Jessica could see it, all shivery and ripply and broken into shiny little pieces.

"If the moon had fallen into the sea…"

Jessica thought of her stories tossing among the dark and silver waves.

Then she looked up. The moon was still in the sky, looking down at her. Was that a smile she saw on its round face?

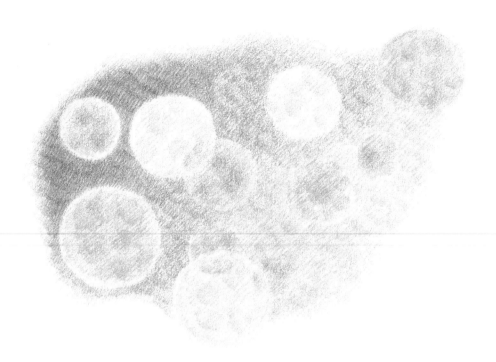

Jessica walked on. Perhaps she'd find the story of this broken moon when she found her other stories.

When Jessica came to the trees, it was very, very dark. The branches hung low and didn't let the moon's light touch the ground.

Jessica didn't have any stories in her head—no scary stories about goblins or banshees or shadows-in-the night—so she wasn't a bit afraid. She walked for a long, long time through the dark trees, looking for a way to the moon. She had just begun to wonder if she were lost too, when she came to a meadow in a little clearing.

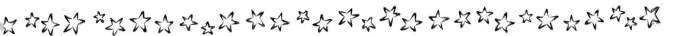

Into the meadow, the moonlight came straight down, so thick and yellow that she could touch it. Right away, Jessica knew that she was getting close to her stories. Or maybe she had already walked into one. There was a tickly sort of magic feeling inside her.

Jessica walked carefully all around the moonpath. The moonbeams looked like clear, golden marshmallows, soft as dandelion fluffs. They floated and bounced lightly about in the air.

Jessica put one foot into the moonpath. Her foot began to float slowly up.

Jessica stepped right into the moonpath.
Immediately she felt as light as moonglow.
Moonbeams bounced against her nose,
and danced beneath her toes.

Jessica began to rise. Half-floating,
half-climbing, she moved farther and farther
up into the sky. Sometimes she'd grab
a big moonbeam and it would bounce
her way up high.

She climbed for a long, long time.

The light about her got brighter and whiter
until suddenly she touched something hard.
She looked up. Jessica was just under the moon.
    Jessica hoped very much that Moon wouldn't
mind. She pulled herself up by a cloud of
whiskers and stood there quietly. Moon was much
bigger than she had thought he would be,
and she felt a bit small and shy, standing there
on his chin. The night was deep and black and
too big to look at.

21

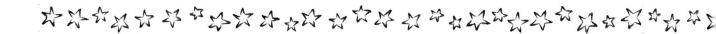

Jessica did not know how to talk to a moon.
His ear seemed very far away. In a polite shout
she began, "Sir Moon, if you please…"

"And thank you," said Moon in a big boomy
voice before she could say anything more.
His voice began as a deep rumble, then rippled
into space like silver bells.

Jessica sat down on his chin and offered Moon
some tea and cookies.

Moon liked the tea, and he liked the night,
and he knew a lot, he said. They talked about
meteorites, and rockets, and where the sun goes
at night, and how a star dances on five toes.

Jessica was having a wonderful time. But Moon
didn't once mention stories.

At last Jessica asked timidly, "Moon, have you
found any lost stories?"

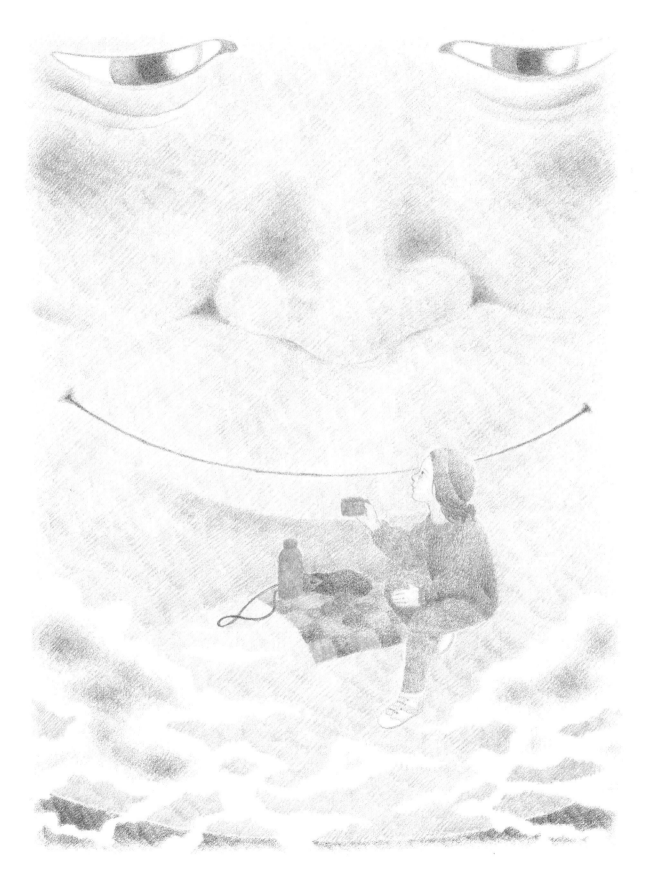

Well, Moon rolled his eyes. And Moon wiggled his ears. And Moon began to smile. His smile grew and G r e w and G R E W, until it covered half his face. Jessica began to worry about falling in.

"Great galloping galaxies! I've been waiting for you," Moon said. "I haven't had a moment's rest! Those stories have been bouncing all night and all day. Drums and dragons and fairies and frogs, fish with hats, and I don't know what else— all talking at once, and falling into each other!

"Clamshells and princes and car rides are all mixed together! I hope you've come to take them home."

Jessica clapped her hands
and jumped up at once.
She suddenly heard a bubbly stream
of laughter and chatter coming
from behind Moon's left ear.

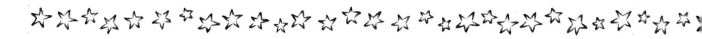

She followed the sound. There, on the other side of the moon, were all her stories, rolling about, a great giggling tangle of arms and paws and magic and trees.

There was *Raven* and *Mouse*, and *The Berry Hunt*, and *The Birthday Party*, and all the stories she had ever heard or been part of.

She untangled each story carefully, and gently put them back into her head.

They snuggled up all warm and cosy and murmured happy little things to each other.

26

Jessica looked at the night. All the stars were beaming, blue and red and yellow and green. And a lovely Moonbird came to fly her down, softly through a haze of moonlight. It landed her right in the little meadow.

Jessica began to walk home. She had to walk
through the dark trees. All the scary stories she
knew woke up and began to whisper frightening
things to her, and she was afraid of the darkness.

But then all the bright, happy stories woke
up too. They began to sing songs to her.
They made the dark woods shine with their singing,
and all the colours of the stars hung on the trees
to show her the way.

Jessica passed the moon that lay broken in the water. She laughed when she remembered the story. It would be a good one to tell to her sister in the morning.

At last she was home. Standing on the beach, she stopped to look up at the night sky. She called a soft good night to Moon.

The lamps were still burning low in the cabin when Jessica tiptoed in. She crawled up into her bed in the loft and lay down. She smiled to herself, a big, happy moon-smile.

Far away, through the mists of moonglow, Jessica thought she could hear the tinkle of starlight and the flutter of Moonbird wings as she floated into sleep.

the end